This igloo book belongs to:

....

igloobooks

Published in 2017
by Igloo Books Ltd, Cottage Farm, Sywell, NN6 0BJ
www.igloobooks.com

Illustrated by Albert Pinilla
Written by Alice King

Cover designed by Lee Italiano
Interiors designed by Justine Ablett & Lee Italiano
Edited by Hannah Cather

LEO002 0217
2 4 6 8 10 9 7 5 3
ISBN 978-1-78557-377-4

Printed and manufactured in China

Little Bears' Picnic
igloobooks

You and me.

Into the woods.

Over the stream.

Up the hill...

... and down again.

Through stormy weather.

Under our umbrella.

We're nearly there.

Almost time for...

... Little Bears' picnic!